ICKY RICKY 1

TOILET PAPER MUMMY

-RIBBIT!

Written & illustrated by

MICHAEL REX

A STEPPING STONE BOOK™

Random House 🏠 New York

To Bob, who some say is a slob,
but I know him as a friend.

Copyright © 2013 by Michael Rex

All rights reserved. Published in the United States by
Random House Children's Books, a division of Random House, Inc., New York.

Random House and the colophon are registered trademarks and
A Stepping Stone Book and the colophon are trademarks of Random House, Inc.

Visit us on the Web!
SteppingStonesBooks.com
randomhouse.com/kids

Educators and librarians, for a variety of teaching tools,
visit us at RHTeachersLibrarians.com

Library of Congress Cataloging-in-Publication Data
Rex, Michael.
Toilet paper mummy / written and illustrated by Michael Rex.
p.   cm. — (Icky Ricky ; #1)
"A Stepping Stone Book."
Summary: Icky Ricky finds his way into all sorts of messes, from having
a sleepover on the ceiling, to launching his pet hot dog into his father's
toolbox, to being shot with his favorite food, Cheese-in-a-Can.
ISBN 978-0-307-93167-2 (pbk.) — ISBN 978-0-375-97101-3 (lib. bdg.) —
ISBN 978-0-307-97538-6 (ebook)
[1. Behavior—Fiction. 2. Humorous stories.] I. Title.
PZ7.R32875Tnm 2013
[E]—dc23   2012025090

Printed in the United States of America

10 9 8 7 6 5 4 3 2 1

CONTENTS

"Ricky! What is that on your face?" asked Icky Ricky's teacher, Ms. Jay.

"It's my homework," said Ricky.

"It looks like cheese!" said Ms. Jay.

"It *is* cheese!" said Ricky.

"Why, oh why, Ricky, is your homework made out of cheese?" asked Ms. Jay.

"Because I couldn't find my bike helmet!" said Ricky.

"I don't understand," said Ms. Jay.

Yesterday, Gus came over to my house and wanted to go bike riding. I couldn't find my bike helmet. So instead of wasting time looking for it, I decided to make one.

I brought a watermelon from the kitchen out to the front steps. I cut it in half with a plastic knife because I'm not allowed to use real knives. That took forever. Then I scooped out all the insides. I put the watermelon on my head. It looked really cool. Then Gus wanted a watermelon helmet, too. So we made his from the other half of the watermelon.

We didn't know if the helmets were safe for bike riding, so we tested them. We dropped things on them, like a book, *splop!* And a shoe, *clomp!* And a wrench, *blonk!* And then a really big book, *kasplop!* Then we did one more test. We ran into a wall as hard as we could.

The helmets cracked, and the juices and gunk ran all over our faces. We couldn't go bike riding.

All that testing had made us hungry. We went back to the steps and scraped the watermelon insides into a bowl. But there were ants in the insides now, and a leaf and a stick. I don't eat ants. (It's not fair to them.) We let the ants have the watermelon, and we picked out the seeds.

WATERMELON SEEDS!
↓ ↓ ↓

ANT!
↓

We decided to have a seed-spitting
contest. We spit our first seeds across the
lawn but couldn't find them in the grass.
Gus figured the seeds would be easier to
find inside, so we went to my room. At
first we weren't very good, and the seeds
went all over the place. One went into
the fishbowl, one went under my sheets,
and one stuck to a lightbulb. We needed
targets. I took all my homework papers
from my folder and drew monsters and
aliens and stuff on them. We spit and spit
and spit.

DOINK

We got really good and could hit the
targets right between the eyes from all the
way out in the hallway. We were awesome.

9

We got tired of spitting seeds since we were experts now, so Gus did a trick for me. He turned his eyelids inside out so I could see the pink side. It was freaking me out.

I was like, "You're freaking me out!"

And Gus said, "Am I *totally* freaking you out?"

Then I told him, "Yes, you're *totally* freaking me out!"

Gus said, "How much am I freaking you out?"

And I was like, "You're freaking me out so much that . . . that . . . I have to blow a booger bubble!" So I blew the biggest booger bubble I could, and we cracked up all over the place.

Gus went home, and I had to do my homework. I'd used all my paper for the seed targets. (I looked for clean sheets of paper but I couldn't find any.) Then I started to think real hard. What else could I write on? What else is smooth and bright and flat? I thought the walls or my bedroom door would be good, but I couldn't get them to school in my backpack.

Then I figured out that cheese would work. First I tried to write on it with a pencil, but the pencil ripped it up. So I ate that slice. Then I tried a crayon, but that just smushed the cheese and didn't really show up. So I ate that slice. Then I tried a marker. That worked. It smeared a little, but if I blew on the cheese, it dried pretty well. The marker was like . . .

I did my homework and filled nine pieces of cheese. I used the last slice of cheese to make a sign that said "Ricky is Awesome!" Then I stuck it to my wall. It stayed, even without tape or glue. Then I went to bed.

I woke up late, and my mom was telling me to hurry. I went to put the homework in my backpack, but it was stuck to my desk. I tried to peel the cheese off my desk, but it just ripped. I used a flyswatter to scrape the slices off and stuck them in my folder. One got all rolled up, but I was able to fix it.

HURRY UP!

My mom was yelling, "C'mon, Ricky! You'll miss the bus! You'll be late for school!" So I had to leave without eating breakfast.

On the bus I was getting really, really hungry. I didn't want to eat my lunch, because then I wouldn't have lunch at lunchtime. So I started to eat the cheese, even though it was my homework. At first I couldn't even taste the marker, but after two slices it got kind of gross. Then Gus was like, "What are you eating?"

I told him I was eating homework cheese.

And then Stew was like "Hey, I love cheese. Can I try homework cheese?"

So Gus and Stew tried a slice of homework cheese. They didn't like it. We bit holes in the cheese and made bank robber masks. They stuck to our faces without any strings or anything.

Gus still had some watermelon seeds
in his pockets, so then we decorated the
masks and made them look even cooler.

I'M GONNA ROB A HUGE BANK AND YOU CAN'T STOP ME! HA! HA! HA!
I'M THE ROBBER THAT ROBS ROBBERS! HEH! HEH! HEH!

"Don't they look cool, Ms. Jay?" Ricky asked.

"Yes, Ricky, they look cool," Ms. Jay said. "It seems like you really tried to do your homework. Do it tonight, and I will accept it."

"I don't know if I can do it tonight," said Ricky.

"Why not?" asked Ms. Jay.

"Because," said Ricky . . .

I'M ALL OUT OF CHEESE!

ICKY RICKY'S TIME-SAVING TIP #1

SNACKS!

Life can get really busy, and you need food to give you energy. I always have a snack on hand so I don't get slowed down.

Spaghetti is a great snack. It's easy to make, fun to eat, and fits into any size pocket! You can even ball it up and keep it in your sock or your hat.

THAT'S NOT HAIR!

If spaghetti seems dull for a snack, spice it up with a meatball and extra tomato sauce. Meatballs and sauce also fit well into most any pocket!

For the kid on the go, spaghetti is the answer!

And remember, kids, plastic is bad for the earth and harmful to the environment. Skip the plastic bags and stuff this yummy treat anywhere you can. You'll be ready for a fun-filled, high-energy, spaghetti-powered day!

Mean Dean was walking right toward Ricky. "Dude, why are you covered with yellow paint, and why do you have baloney and dog hair all over you?" he asked in his mean voice.

"That's a long story, Dean," said Ricky.

Dean's little sister, Samantha, came up behind Ricky.

"Why are you wearing that stupid hat, and where is my remote-controlled car?" Dean asked her angrily.

Samantha looked at Ricky. She was about to cry.

Ricky started to explain, "That's what I was going to tell you about, Dean. . . ."

Samantha came over to my house this morning, trying to sell her toys. She was like, "I drove my brother's remote-controlled car into Black Pond, and I need money to buy him a new one. Do you want to buy some of my toys?" But all she had were girls' toys, like Glitter Pony Superstar, Pinky Pink Pals, Poo-Poo Cutie Kittens, and Poo-Poo Cutie Kitten Babies. I didn't have any money anyway, so I asked her if she wanted me to try to get the RC car out of the pond for her, and she was like, "Yes! Yes!"

We went down to the pond, and she
showed me where the car drove off the
footbridge. We looked real hard from the
bridge, but the water in that pond is so
black and scummy that you can't see the
bottom. I walked around to the side of the
bridge and stepped into the pond.

I kept my shoes on, because I know a lot of people throw junk and garbage in the water. One time I saw a whole air conditioner in there, and another time I saw a kid throw in a notebook on the last day of school.

I walked through the water to where Samantha was pointing, and I started to feel around. I pulled something out! It was an old baseball glove. I was like, "Cool! I'm keeping this." Then with my other hand, I pulled out an old can of soda, and it wasn't even opened. I stuffed it into my pocket to keep for later. I kept digging around and finding all these cool things, like an old windshield wiper, a deflated soccer ball, a CD, and a baseball hat. But I couldn't find the car. I put my head underwater to look for it, but the water was too dirty.

Something tickled my leg. I reached in and pulled out a frog. I asked Sam if she wanted to give the frog to you, but she said you would still want your RC car. I closed my eyes, bent down, and felt around one more time. I grabbed something, stood up, and yanked. Whatever it was, it was really stuck. I pulled and pulled, but it wouldn't move. I needed both hands but I didn't want to lose the frog, and Samantha wouldn't hold it, so I put it in my mouth. I didn't bite it or anything, I just held it with my lips. I put both hands on the thing I was pulling and tugged really hard.

It yanked free and shot into the air.
It was underwear! Huge underwear! Huge,
old, pond-scum underwear! It flew into
the sky and blocked the sun! It was an
underwear eclipse! The frog freaked and
jumped out of my mouth and landed on
Samantha's head. She started screaming
like crazy! Then the underwear landed on
my head, like, *splat!*

OOOSH!

Dean interrupted Ricky. "Dude, this story is stupid. What's it got to do with my remote-controlled car?"

"Just wait," said Ricky, "there's more!"

TO BE CONTINUED . . .

"Ricky!" his mom cried as she walked into his bedroom. "Why are you guys sleeping on the ceiling?"

"Because we ate too much junk food!" said Ricky.

"That makes no sense," said his mom.

"Sure it does," said Ricky. "Let me explain. . . ."

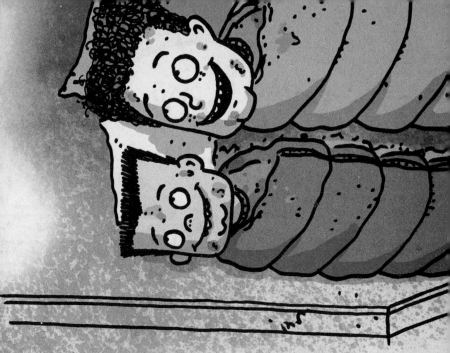

Last night, when Gus and Stew came over for our sleepover, the first thing we did was get out all the food we had. We had chips, pickles, candy bars, peanut butter, ketchup, juice, popcorn, pizza, and Cheese-in-a-Can. This was a great way to start a sleepover.

We started watching monster movies. First we saw a vampire movie. We put ketchup in our mouths, and when the vampires bit people, we let it dribble out.

THERE'S NO WAY TO GET AWAY FROM A BLOOD-THIRSTY VAMPIRE!
I'M THE VAMPIRE THAT BITES VAMPIRES!

A monster movie came on about a big
spider that spun giant webs and trapped
all these people. It was pretty lame, so we
decided it would be better in 3-D. I hid
behind the TV while Gus and Stew watched.
Every time the spider made his web, I shot
the Cheese-in-a-Can at Gus and Stew. It was
great, and it made the movie awesome. At
first Gus and Stew dodged the spray, but
then they tried to see if they could catch it
in their mouths.

That movie ended and a space movie came on. We made that 3-D, too. Every time someone shot a laser, I sprayed the cheese again. There were asteroids in this movie. We used popcorn to make that part 3-D. We chucked it all over the place when the asteroids were shooting through space. We noticed that the popcorn stuck anywhere there was Cheese-in-a-Can cheese, even to our shirts.

Then we started throwing popcorn at each other, and the person with the most popcorn on his shirt was the loser, so we tried to eat the popcorn when no one was looking.

But we didn't have any more Cheese-in-a-Can, so we covered our shirts with peanut butter and tossed more popcorn at each other. It was awesome.

We ran out of popcorn, so we decided
to see if the pickles would stick to our
shirts. I chucked one at Stew and *plop*,
it fell on the floor. They were too heavy,
so we ate a few and had Pickle Olympics.
We did the pickle toss, pickle soccer,
pickle hacky sack, and then freestyle pickle
gymnastics.

That was the easiest. All you had to
do was move your body all crazy and stuff
while holding a pickle in your mouth.

We kept eating the chips and the candy bars and any popcorn we could find. The peanut-butter-covered popcorn was better than the Cheese-in-a-Can-covered popcorn. But we all started feeling like we were going to barf. We had eaten too much junk food. I really felt like barf was coming up my throat. Stew said my brain wouldn't let me barf on my favorite toy, so he held it in front of my face. And you know what? I didn't barf! It was like magic. We needed to feel better, so I said we should eat something healthy, like soup.

We snuck down to the kitchen to make
soup. None of us had ever made soup, so we
just started grabbing things that might be in
soup and put them all in a bowl. We found an
onion, a carrot, some beans, some broccoli,
and a mango. We looked for a potato but
couldn't find one, so we used frozen French
fries. Soup should have some meat, so we put
in a fish stick.

I found my bike helmet in the freezer. I put it back in there so I could stay cool the next time I went biking.

We tried stirring all the soup stuff in the bowl, but it wasn't getting soupy. Gus said we should mash it up, so we put it in a plastic bag and whacked it with spoons.

We were making too much noise, so we
went back to my room. We kept trying to
mash the stuff up, but it still wasn't soupy.
We poured in the leftover pickle juice to
make it soupier. We put the bag between
some books and smushed it. We put it
under my mattress and rolled on it. Finally,
Stew stood on it and that worked a little.
Then I had my best idea of the night.

I put the bag on the floor and climbed up on my dresser. I jumped as high as I could and came down hard on the soup bag. It exploded! The soup gunk shot all over Gus, all over Stew, and all over the wall and the floor. It was awesome!

We tasted the soup, but it wasn't very good. We were all pretty tired by now, so we got out our sleeping bags, but the floor was so totally covered with soup gunk and popcorn and pickles and ketchup and cheese that there was nowhere to put them. I was trying to think where else we could sleep. Maybe in the basement? Maybe outside? Maybe in the attic? Then I had the perfect idea.

WHAT ABOUT THE CEILING?

We covered our sleeping bags with lots of peanut butter, tons of ketchup, and anything else sticky we could find. We tossed the sleeping bags up to the ceiling, and they stuck. Then we climbed onto my desk, across my dresser, and into the bags.

Right before we fell asleep, we started to make a list of all the foods that should come in a can, like Tacos-in-a-Can and Pizza-in-a-Can and Pickles-in-a-Can and Toast-in-a-Can and Homework-Cheese-in-a-Can. And then we fell asleep. That's why we are sleeping on the ceiling.

"Oh . . . okay," said Mom. "Come on down, and I'll make some breakfast."

"That's okay," said Ricky. "We thought of that last night and stuck the pizza to the ceiling, too."

THERE'S NOTHING LIKE BREAKFAST IN BED!

CLEANING YOUR ROOM!

Cleaning your room is a big drag and eats up valuable kid time. That's why I keep my room organized alphabetically.

"**A**" items, such as airplane parts, art supplies, and antique sandwiches, go "All over."

"**B**" items, such as baseball gloves, balloons, and baboon costumes, go "Beneath everything else."

KEEP A LIST SO YOU KNOW WHERE THINGS ARE.

"C" items, such as clothes, cookies, and collectibles, get stuffed in the "Closet."

And "D" items, such as dinosaur toys, dishes, and dirty socks, are "Dumped in drawers."

Get it? Let this handy-dandy tip keep you organized so you have time to play with your friends, explore the bottom of a pond, and send pizza to your pen pal in Japan!

Mean Dean was staring at Samantha and Ricky. "I still don't know why you are covered with all that yellow paint, and I still don't have my car."

"Well, just listen," said Ricky. . . .

We gave up trying to find the car in the pond, and Samantha was about to cry, so I said I would help her get money for a new one. We realized that selling toys wouldn't work, because only kids want toys, but kids don't have money. We needed something adults would buy. Then I had a great idea! "Why don't we set up a lemonade stand?" I said, and Samantha said, "Yes," and we ran back to my house.

We found one little packet of lemonade mix in the kitchen. We mixed it up fast, but didn't read the directions and put in too much water. It didn't taste lemony enough, so we searched around and found some lemon cough drops and put them in. They looked like little lemon ice cubes. It tasted better, but not quite right, so we stirred in some sugar. Now it was too thick, and I was like, "Man, making lemonade is hard," and then I had my best idea of the day. The soda I found in the pond was lemon-lime! I poured it in. It tasted awesome!

We ran to the garage and found some
yellow paint. Samantha made signs and
I set up a little table. It looked excellent,
but no one bought any lemonade. We were
screaming our guts out, like, "Lemonade,
lemonade, get your ice-cold lemonade!" But
still no one bought any.

I held one of the signs up high for
people to see, and I got some yellow paint
on me and that gave me an idea. I grabbed
the paint from the garage and started
painting all over my face, my arms, my

shirt, and my pants. Then I found an old
football helmet and painted that yellow, too.
Samantha painted a little kid cowboy hat
to wear. I was like, "I'll be the Lemonade
Man!" I looked really cool, and then I started
dancing around on the sidewalk and shaking
my butt and stuff and singing,

We still sold nothing. Samantha said we had to have a gimmick to sell the lemonade, and I asked, "Like what?" She said maybe we could give away a free straw with each cup. I thought that was a great idea. I ran to the kitchen and looked around. No straws. I was thinking that maybe I could make straws. I needed something thin that I could roll up. Baloney! Yes!

① ← SLICE OF BALONEY

② ROLLED UP

③ BALONEY STRAW!

THREE CHEERS FOR BALONEY!

I ran back to the table with some baloney and showed Samantha how to make a baloney straw. We made a bunch and put them in the cups. We had a few extra slices so I stuck them on my shirt like polka dots. Again, we sold nothing!

Then I had my second-best idea of the day! "We should sell door to door!" I said, and we grabbed some cups and straws and started ringing people's doorbells. Everyone was like, "No, thank you," and then they closed the door in my face before I even did my Lemonade Man dance.

Finally, the man at the end of the
street said "Yes" to the lemonade, but
he didn't want a baloney straw. He was
getting his money when all of a sudden his
big dog came running to the door, jumped
up, and snatched the baloney polka dots.
I got knocked down off the stoop, and the
lemonade and baloney straws spilled all
over me! I was lucky I had my helmet on.

The dog jumped on top of me and started gobbling up the baloney, and his dog hair was sticking to the paint, and his slobber was flying all over the place!

"Ricky!" shouted Ricky's dad as he came around the corner of the house and saw Ricky, Gus, and Stew. "Why did a hot dog with a mustache fall out of the sky and into my toolbox?"

"Because it was his birthday wish!" said Ricky.

"Whose birthday wish?" asked Dad.

"Harry's," said Ricky.

"Who is Harry?" asked Ricky's dad.

"He's my pet hot dog, and I'm glad you found him!" said Ricky.

"Ricky," said his dad quietly, "start from the beginning."

"All right . . ."

I woke up today and realized it was Harry's birthday. I looked all over for him, and then I remembered that I left him in the hamper ("H" for "Hamper," "H" for "Harry"), so I dug around and there he was, under a dirty dish I used for eating a hamburger. It had been so long since I had seen him that he had grown hair!

BEFORE!

The first thing I needed to do for his birthday was give him a haircut. I used Mom's fancy little makeup scissors to snip away most of the fuzz.

Part of the hair I couldn't cut away. It looked like a funky beard. But if you have a funky beard, you need a funky mustache. I reached between my toes and picked some fuzz, then I stuck my finger in my ear to get some earwax. I used the earwax to stick the toe fuzz to his face, like an awesome mustache. Then I redrew his eyes. He looked ready to party.

Once that was done, I had to figure
out what to get Harry for his birthday.
I looked around the house for ideas. I've
lost Harry a few times. Once I lost him in
my backpack, once he fell behind the toilet,
and once I left him outside overnight. *That's
it*, I thought. *I'll build him his own house so I can't
ever lose him again.*

I grabbed some old shoe boxes, some scissors, some paints, and some glitter. I cut the box and made a house with two rooms. Then I painted the walls and poured glitter on them. But I didn't have any glue. How was I going to stick all this together?

I thought, *Mayonnaise looks like glue! I'll use that.* I got some mayonnaise from the fridge and brushed it all over the hot dog house. It began to fall apart. I needed to find something stickier. Maple syrup! I grabbed some from the kitchen and squirted it all over the house. The syrup held Harry's house together, and it was looking pretty cool.

The house needed a TV. Somewhere
in my room I had a little TV-shaped pencil
sharpener. I crawled under my bed and
shoved some junk around. Finally, I found
it. I also found a cookie that I lost in the

first grade. The bad thing was, I was
covered with syrup and mayonnaise and
paint, and the dust fuzz from under my bed
was stuck all over me.

I sneezed over and over. I tried to cover
my mouth, but my hand was all painty and
covered with syrup. Dust fuzz is the one thing
I don't like because it makes me sneezy and
makes my nose drip boogers like crazy. Now I
would have to take a bath before the party.

I was thinking that I would invite Gus and Stew to the party. I could make really fancy invitations with the glitter and stuff. But that was a waste of time. I opened the window and just shouted,

HEY, GUYS! COME OVER FOR A PARTY IN ONE HOUR!

I only had an hour and a whole ton of stuff to do. I had to wash my clothes, take a bath, make sandwiches, and bake a cake. I didn't know if I could do it all, but then I saw my cheese sign that said "Ricky is Awesome!" and I knew I could do it!

When you think about it, it doesn't make any sense to wash your clothes in one place, and wash your body in another place, and make lunch in another place.

Right? So I decided to do them all at once.
I grabbed the peanut butter and the jelly
and a few slices of bread and potato chips,
cookies, and some jelly beans. I brought
them into the bathroom. I filled up the tub.
Then I jumped in with my clothes on and
laid out the food on the side of the tub.

I didn't have enough bowls and plates, so I had the great idea of putting everything in a sandwich. Since I forgot to bring a knife to spread the peanut butter and jelly, I used a toy hammerhead shark that I keep in the bathtub. I was kind of splashing around and the bread was getting wet when I knocked the chips into the tub.

I scooped up the chips. I got some of the dust fuzz that was floating around in the water, too, but I didn't think anyone would notice. I crumbled the cookies on

top of the peanut butter and jelly, put the jelly beans on, and put on another slice of bread. The sandwiches looked awesome.

A slice of bread fell in the tub and floated around. I stood up, aimed my shark, and dropped my shark on it.

KASPLASH!

It tore a perfect hole right through the bread. I splashed around some more in the water to make sure I was clean, and I stepped out of the tub.

By accident, I knocked the sandwiches onto the floor. Those sandwiches were sure taking a beating! I picked them up and tried to dry them with the toilet paper. It just stuck to them. And to me. Actually it was kind of cool. I stuck some toilet paper to my belly and started spinning around and around. Soon I looked like a mummy. What an awesome way to look for a birthday party. Then I was like,

OH NO! I FORGOT TO MAKE A CAKE!

I ran to the kitchen. I found a box of cake mix and some icing. The directions on the box said the cake takes forty-five minutes to cook! Forty-five minutes? Yeah, right! I only had five. I had to think fast. I poured the cake-mix powder into a big bowl. Then I scooped the icing into the bowl. I mushed it all up with my hands and made it into a tube shape. It didn't really look like a cake. It looked like a log. So I called it the cake-log-thing. I tried to write "Happy Birthday" on it with mustard, but I ran out of room. It only said "Happy Birt."

CAKE-LOG-THING

Gus and Stew came over, and they
wanted to be toilet paper mummies, too.
They ran to the bathroom, jumped in the
tub, got soaked, and then got all rolled up.
We started jumping around and playing air
guitar, mummy-style.

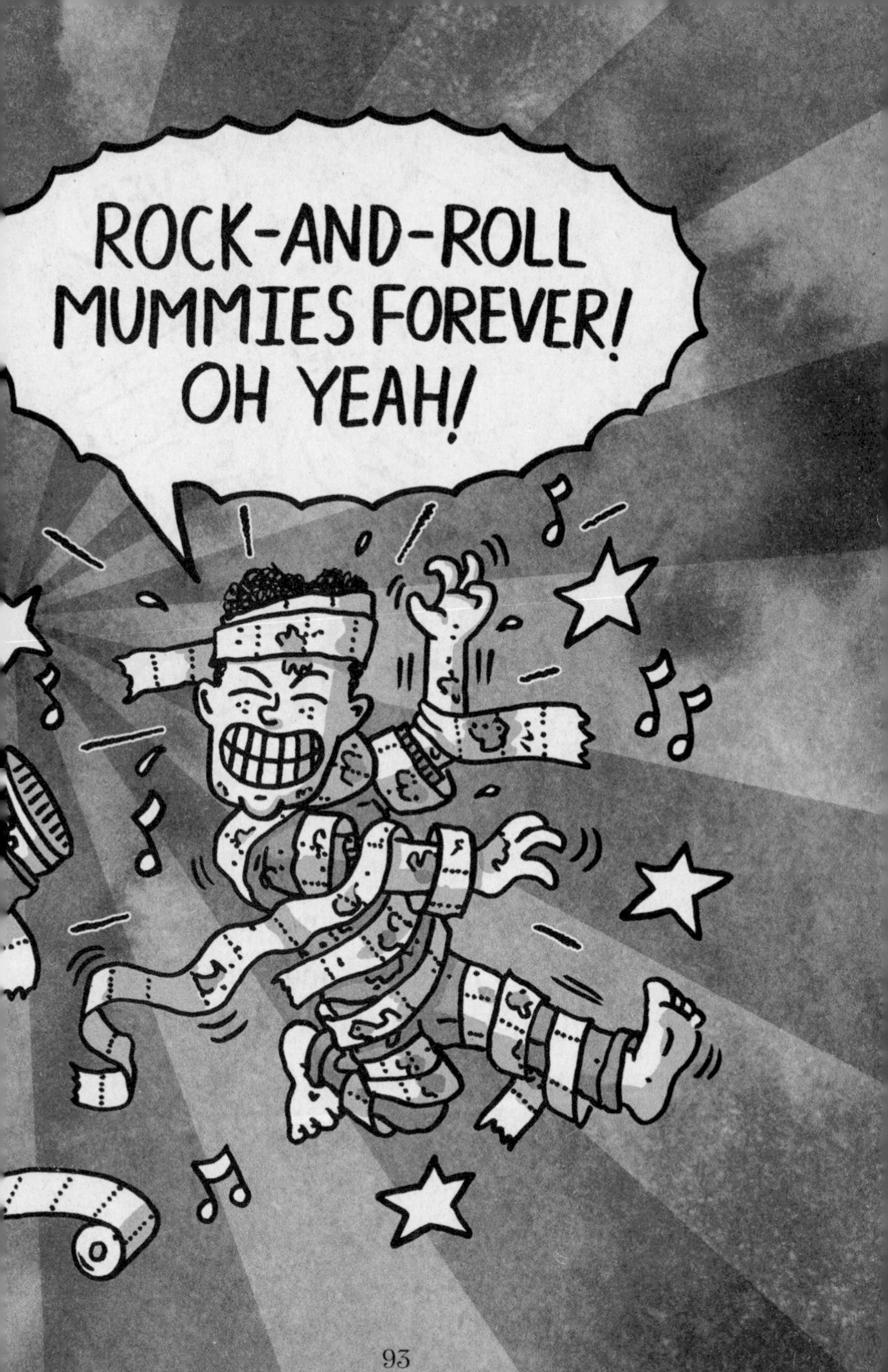
ROCK-AND-ROLL MUMMIES FOREVER! OH YEAH!

This was turning into the best party
ever. We tried to eat the sandwiches, but
they had gotten too soggy and toilet-papery
and fell apart. The jelly beans were still
good so we picked those out and ate them.
We ran around the house as mummies for
a while, but then we got thinking about
candy and hitting things and wanted to do
the piñata. Every party has a piñata!

THE PIÑATA!
HOW COULD I FORGET
THE PIÑATA?

We needed to make a piñata. I looked
around the house for something strong
enough to hold stuff but that would break
with a stick. I took one of Mom's garbage
bags. The box says that they are strong
and tough, but Mom rolls her eyes and says
they're cheapo and always rip.

We ran to the kitchen to fill the bag with candy. First we dropped in the few jelly beans that were left, but that hardly filled the bag. We needed something else. We added the leftover cookies.

The bag still wasn't full. Gus had some watermelon seeds in his pocket so he put them in. We opened the fridge. What else could go in the piñata?

Gus was like, "Salami?"
And I was like, "No."
Stew was like, "Frozen waffles?"
And I was like, "No."
Then Gus was like, "Celery?"
And I was like, "No."
And then Stew was like, "Eggs?"
And I was like,

We love eggs! Gus loves fried eggs. Stew loves scrambled eggs. I love poached eggs.

We decided the eggs looked kind of boring and white, so we drew faces and stuff on them with markers. Only three broke, which we thought was pretty good.

Then we put them in the bag and tied the top. We drew a big face on the bag to make it look more like a piñata. Then I put an old baseball hat on it and some broken sunglasses. He was looking awesome.

Gus held him up and said, "It's Señor Piñata Dude!"

And then Stew said, *"¡Buenos dias, Señor!"*

And I said, *"¿Dondé esta el Queso-en-una-Lata?"* which means "Where is the Cheese-in-a-Can?" I think.

Then I found some string and tied it to the top of the bag, and we were done. We ran outside and tied one end of the string to a branch, and then we each grabbed a stick.

We were gonna take turns and be all polite and stuff, but we were having so much fun that we all started swinging and smacking Señor Piñata Dude like crazy. The cheap bag exploded, and the eggs shot out, and the jelly beans flew in the air, and the cookie crumbs and watermelon seeds stuck all over us. We laughed so hard that we rolled in the yard, and the eggy goop picked up leaves and sticks and dirt.

But you know what? I was a horrible
party thrower. We never gave Harry his
cake, and he never even got a shot at his
piñata. So I went inside and got him and
the cake-log-thing. We sang "Happy Birt"
to Harry, and we ate the cake-log-thing.
It wasn't that bad, unless you bit into a big
chunk of powder mix. Then I asked Harry
what his birthday wish was. Stew and Gus
were like, "Dude, hot dogs can't talk."

And I was like,

Then we were cracking up again, and
we decided that since all of us wished we
could fly, then Harry must want to fly, too!

We tied him to the piñata
string and started swinging
him around and around and
around. It's really hard to tie
a string to a hot dog, and he
slipped out of the knot and
shot off over the house.

WHOOOOOOOOOOOOOOOOOOOSH!!

"See, Dad? It makes total sense," Ricky said.

"I'm very disappointed, Ricky," his father said.

"I'm sorry I made such a mess in the bathroom," said Ricky.

"It's not that," said his father.

"I'm sorry I made such a mess in the kitchen," said Ricky.

"It's not that, either, Ricky," said his father.

"I'm sorry I made such a mess in the backyard," said Ricky.

"It's not that, either, Ricky," said his father. "I'm disappointed that you threw this wonderful party for Harry, and you didn't even invite Pete."

ICKY RICKY'S TIME-SAVING TIP #3

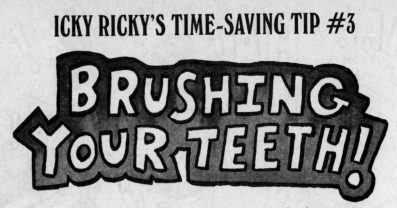

BRUSHING YOUR TEETH!

Kids need to brush their teeth, but we don't always have the time. Kids are busy people. Between school, homework, and playing, who has time to brush three times a day?

I BARELY HAVE TIME TO CHANGE MY UNDERWEAR!

That's why I put a little toothpaste into every meal. I mix a tiny bit in with my cereal in the morning. Just a smidge works as a tasty sandwich spread at lunch, and a pea-sized glob as a treat at dinner!

When I'm done with my meal, my teeth are clean, and my breath is fresh!

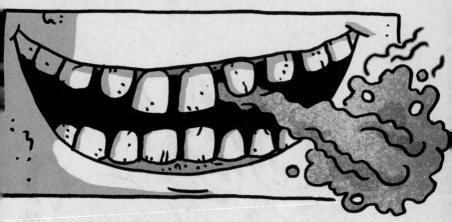

Not only that, but I'm not wasting water by brushing. And I'm not polluting the environment by throwing away old toothbrushes!

It leaves me lots of time to work on my new cookbook, too:

101 Awesome Dishes to Make with Cheese-in-a-Can!

#37, CHEESE-IN-A-CAN PANCAKES!

"Well," Ricky told Mean Dean, "we don't have your car. But the man gave us five dollars for the lemonade and all the baloney his dog ate. It's yours now." Ricky handed the money to Dean.

"RC cars cost way more than five dollars!" said Dean as his face grew red.

"I'm sorry for losing your car," said Samantha.

Dean was furious! "I told you not to borrow it! I knew you'd ruin it or mess it up. I didn't think you'd crash it into a pond!"

"I said I'm sorry. I didn't mean to lose it," said Samantha, and she started to cry.

"I don't care!" Dean yelled. "You know what I'm going to do? I'm going to go up to your room, get your dolls, and throw them in Black Pond."

"What?" cried Samantha.

"If I can't have my car, you can't have your dolls! Mr. Monkey and Mr. Donkey are going in the pond!" He turned to go back to his house.

"No! No! No! I'm sorry! You can't!"
Samantha grabbed his shirt and tried to
stop him.

"I'm doing it!" shouted Dean.

"Wait!" Ricky broke in.

I DID IT! I LOST YOUR RC CAR!

Dean looked back. "Huh?"

"I was driving it when it went in the
pond . . . not Samantha," said Ricky.

Samantha looked at Ricky. He talked so fast she couldn't get a word in.

"It's my fault," said Ricky. "What are you going to do about it?"

"I can't believe you made my sister lie to me!" said Dean. "She's just a little kid, jerk!" He hugged Samantha. "Don't worry, Samantha, I won't chuck out your dolls." He looked at Ricky. "You're a real creep, Ricky!"

Ricky put on his best guilty face. "Yeah, well, I'm a creep," he said. "I'm the creep who lost your RC car, and I'm the creep covered with dog slobber and yellow paint. I don't know what you're going to do to me, Dean. I really don't. I don't know if you're going to beat me up, throw my stuff in Black Pond, or say mean things about me in school. I just don't know."

Ricky got down on his knees.

JUST PLEASE, PLEASE, PLEASE DO NOT SPRAY ME WITH CHEESE-IN-A-CAN! I CAN'T STAND THAT STUFF! IT'S THE MOST DISGUSTING, HORRIBLE, NASTIEST STUFF IN THE WHOLE WORLD! I GAG WHEN I SMELL IT! I GET A RASH WHEN I TOUCH IT! JUST LOOKING AT IT MAKES ME WANT TO

BARF!

"Dude, you shouldn't have said that!"
said Dean as he ran back to his house.

"Thanks," said Samantha. She smiled
a great big smile at Ricky.

Dean ran back from the house with a
can of Cheese-in-a-Can!

"Oh no! Not Cheese-in-a-Can!" shouted
Ricky. He covered his head. Dean started
spraying the stuff all over him.

"Stop! Stop! I can't stand it!" cried Ricky.
"I'm gagging! I'm gagging! I'm getting sick!
My skin is burning! Stop! Stop!" He rolled
on the ground, and Dean kept showering
him with the cheese. Ricky turned his head
from Dean and looked at Samantha. Dean
couldn't see Ricky laughing!

101 AWESOME DISHES TO MAKE WITH CHEESE-IN-A-CAN! FEATURING...

Cheese-in-a-Can Sandwich

Cheese-in-a-Can Stew

Cheese-in-a-Can Sushi

Grilled Cheese-in-a-Can

Cheese-in-a-Can Cupcakes (the Cheese-in-a-Can is inside!)

and

Cheese-in-a-Can-Covered Honey-Mustard, Chocolate-Syrup Hot Wings!

ICKY · RICKY 2

THE END OF THE WORLD